University of North Texas Press ❖ Denton, Texas

The Journals of

Scheherazade

Poems by

Sheryl St. Germain

10 9 8 7 6 5 4 3 2 1

Permissions

University of North Texas Press
Post Office Box 13856
Denton, Texas 76203

Grateful Acknowledgement is extended to the editors of the
following journals and anthologies where some of these poems first
appeared: *The Abiko Quarterly; Breaking Ground; Cream City Review;
Five Fingers Review; Louisiana Literature; Massachusetts Review;
Negative Capability; New Letters; No Roses Review; OnTheBus;
RiverSedge; Spoon River Poetry Review; The Texas Review* and
A Certain Attitude: Poems by Seven Texas Women.

Library of Congress Cataloging-in-Publication Data

St. Germain, Sheryl.
The journals of Scheherazade : poems / by Sheryl St. Germain.
p.   cm.
ISBN 1-57441-010-5
I. Title.
PS3569.T1223J68   1996
811'.54—dc20   95-39438
CIP

Cover design by Amy Layton

for d.s.,
whose imagination
so inspired me

Table of Contents

3. Eight Nights of Fantasies

4. And a Song from Death

Note

I have always admired the character of Scheherazade: her bravery, her imagination, the erotic, direct nature of the tales she tells. And though she tells tales and I write poems, I feel drawn to her because the writing of the poem for me is a way of staving off death, as were her tales. No more poems, no more ways, however fictional, of understanding life, thus, no more life.

Scheherazade's tales in the *Arabian Nights* are designed for two imagined listeners: her husband-to-be and her younger sister, Dunazade, whose job it is to urge her on in the telling of the tales. The tales are designed to be wondrous; if the husband becomes bored at any time she will lose her life. They are also designed to educate both the husband and the sister; she wants to civilize her husband so that he will not be such a despot, and she wants to teach her sister about social and religious mores; in other words, her tales are instructions about how to live. I like to think of the larger audience of the *Nights*, and of this collection of poems as a collection of lovers and children, roles we have all played at one time or another, the roles in which we are, perhaps, most susceptible to learning, illumination.

The original, unexpurgated *Arabian Nights* has a remarkably erotic flavor. Every night before Scheherazade tells the next tale she and her husband-to-be make love. He doesn't realize it, but he is slowly falling in love with her. The tales are bawdy and sexual, sometimes crudely so, in the manner of *The Canterbury Tales* or *The Decameron*. As if Scheherazade were using the body to seduce the intellect and heart. I find the idea of this kind of eroticism—eroticism in the service of something other than eroticism—fresh and dramatically fascinating.

When I think about what it is I want poems to be, I think of Scheherazade. That the poem always seem to be written or told to a beloved, real or imagined, that it have that kind of intimacy. That the poem be wondrous, lustrous, entertaining in a deep way. That the telling of it be a saving of one's own life, illuminating for real or imagined sisters and brothers, one's extended "family" of readers. That is why I have taken her name in writing these poems, that is why I have imagined myself as a twentieth century Scheherazade, charged with her duties, her intellectual and spiritual lust for the elemental human desires—survival, entertainment, enlightenment.

Like Scheherazade, most of the protagonists . . . save themselves and fulfill their destiny because they can weave the threads of their lives together in narratives. . . . Narration is raised to an art par excellence, *for the nights are paradoxically moments of light, epiphanies, through which the listeners gain insight into the mysteries and predicaments that might otherwise overwhelm them and keep them in darkness. . . . The primary concern of all the major tales is survival through artistic narration that is convincingly wondrous if not miraculous.*

—Jack Zipes, *Afterword to* **Arabian Nights**

1. Stories to Save Herself

Doctrine of Signatures

As if it could help me
when I look at my own face and the big
teeth, large lips, dark eyes, overgrown
eyebrows, the gray hairs settling in,
the skin getting harder, and wonder
what could this face heal, this mouth,
and what should we call it: *liverwort,*
bloodroot, cockscomb, heartsease,
lupine.

Speaking

I am holding a pillow between my thighs
gripped tight as desire all the nights
of my youth. And the pressure feels good,
like love—familiar, sexual,
although I do not yet understand these words;
all that is real is the feel of the pillow
bunched between my legs.

It is the low string to which all else
is deep-tuned. My mother's breasts,
tumbled out to me, her nipples pink
as new flesh from a healing wound;
her perfume, warm, milky, a low whisper;
my father's love of sex, of women;
the music my mother plays at night—
black voices like bruises that cry
into the walls.

It is the beating of my father's heart:
he is looking at my mother
in church, before they are married,
he is watching the movement
of her breasts as she breathes.

It is his wanting, her aching
that fills every corner of the house
until it seems all I can hear
is their blood drumming the veins of us all—
sisters, brothers, children not yet born.

I cannot speak without them.

I cannot speak except with lips that long
for the food of other lips, the liquor
of other bodies; I cannot speak except
with all the hungers and terrors
of the blood that sings me
in this holy, obscene darkness.

Common Time

I am not very good
but I practice diligently,
after school and before
the job at the department store,
as if diligence itself
were a way to the sublime.

The family cannot afford piano lessons,
so a neighbor teaches me for free.
One ta two,
I am learning about sadness, already
the minor chords, the diminished sevenths,
infect me, as if where fingers touch keys
are open wounds,
where a blood or virus
enters to travel
veins and arteries until
it reaches voice.

one ta two ta
brother is dead
three ta four ta
sister is wed

one ta two ta
father falls down
three ta four ta
then he is gone

A note that sounds wrong
could be right, could be more
than right: could be beautiful.
I play the dissonant chords again
and again, how lovely they are,
how like love. Repetition.
ta three

I play melodies with a belief
only a child could have—
there is a heaven,
there are notes to learn to read,
there are measures to count,
ta four ta

Black notes scatter across the page
like something broken.
Memory floods my hands like a god.

One ta two ta
Fingers remember
what I no longer am.
Three ta four ta
Fingers remember
what I no longer can.

My Body in Summer

Not yet calloused, but cut and scarred,
bruised and dirty because I don't
wear gloves, am ungraceful—

I smell like sun, wine,
unstable weather, heavy rains,
peppers from the garden,
grass, new paint, like labor,
sadness, like a mother
who has lost her child,
weeds, tomato vine
ready to break from
the weight of tomatoes,

like broken
fingernails, finger
crescents of dirt, sex
without sex, like when a woman
removes her diaphragm
and smells the mushroom
smell of the gone one,

coconut, ink, despair, fern,
skin-grit, bruises, black flies,
who love my skin, it is a banquet
with its small wounds,
its salt and wine and smoke
smell from the barbecue,
my pungent armpits, fertile

as any forest,
sphagnum moss,
soft rotting wood,
the way river birches bend
until I think I will die of their beauty,

smell of everything I have touched
intimately and everything I have wanted to,
red biting ants, blood mosquitoes,
insect bodies that go flat like love
when we smash them,
all the small terrors we smell of,

hand of beloved,
milk, music and sky,
hope and veins, I am a feast,
a garden, a corpse,
my skin suckled and flayed,

and the late sun's death,
thick and creamy and dark,
covers my skin like a sauce:

from this have you come,
to this shall you return,
take this and eat of it,
this odoriferous perfume,
this blessed sweating body.

Rent

For nothing can be sole or whole
That has not been rent.

                                  Crazy Jane

The hardball came hard and fast,
not unexpected, but surprisingly
cruel to the one who ran,
face uplifted and radiant with joy,
his first baseball game,
arms outstretched as if in love,
just to the place where
his nose would meet the ball
straight on—

I heard the scream, saw him turn
around, the blood spurting out
of both nostrils as if every vein
and capillary in the nose were cut,
the blood pouring down the nose
into his mouth, the mouth filling
with blood and grief, overflowing
to the chin, running down
underneath the Cub Scout shirt,
the dark red splotches turning
the gold neckerchief red
with blood's beauty.

I saw him put his hands to his nose,
cup it, pull one hand away
full of blood, *father take this cup
from me,* and I couldn't move
for a moment, though knowledge
continued to pour and run down his face,
though he looked screaming
at his palm, as if it were
the palm's fault, the blood darker
there and drying a little, now
filling in the fingerprints and life
line.

It is my own hand, after the car accident,
I am in the back seat,
I have put my hand on my father's head
to shake him awake, I have pulled
my hand away, he has not woken.
I am looking at my palm, sticky
with the blood and hair of my father,
all of his mortality foretold
for me there in the blooded palm.

When one breaks a nose,
for that is what my son has done,
the evidence is in the X-ray,
the crack like a lost hair
there in the bone, the invisible
made visible. If only we could
X-ray our souls that way, find
the cracks, the cancers,
the evidence of love—

there, in my father's head,
that crooked line, that's love,
here, this other one, that's regret.

After you know the thing
is broken, there is nothing
to be done, you can only watch
the nose swell and bloom, flatten
and poke out where it shouldn't,
bruise, open and blossom
like a flower that doesn't
want to die, its petals open beyond belief
for days after cutting, as if the very act
of cutting has brought on its most intense beauty.

My son looks at himself in the mirror,
fingers the bruised and broken
thing as if it were a hurt animal.
I think of my father's cracked head,
the palm of blood, the beginning
of knowledge.

My Son's Body

Sometimes he presents his body to me
like a present he knows I want
but will not take—
when he lies almost naked
and asks me to scratch his back,
turns over on his stomach
raises his shirt—

How could I not notice the way
his young rump rises
in his first morning stretch,
the buttocks like hard plums or peaches,
and the small penis
that rises softly, a hesitant flag,
and his almost invisible balls, naked
raisins, tucked in tight—how sweet
his body is, how could I
not notice, how could I not understand
wanting to have it, to touch it
not as a mother but as the beloved,
how could I not understand
thinking to enter into that beauty,
forgetting the way possession
turns everything it wants
into itself.

There are times when the line
we draw between one thing and another
cuts through like righteousness,
there it is,
we can hold it, see it.

Other times lines fade,
like bruises and youth—
and not seeing,
one cannot distinguish between
love and *love*.

Some of us are lost already
when the line's shadow calls out
from somewhere, like a poem,
too late.

Abortion

I will carry the knowledge of it
forever in my body. No,
no, I say clearly, the weight
of no in me like a sound
without end, the long open *oh*
of it—*no* doesn't end like
yes, it stays open, spreads
into every corner of your life,
fills you with sound
until you are swollen,
have long forgotten the beginning
of the word, when all that's left
is the open vowel, the weight,
the joyless wisdom, ooooooh.

Ereshkigal

That the egg within me
pulsing with life should
cause the earth to split
and I to be pulled into
that darker world of my own making.

it is home of a woman
who seems sister to me
black with rage, leeches
for hair, her mouth a
wound never meant to heal
full and rich with the blood
of those before me

And when I stop the almost-
child inside me she comes
inside instead, fitting
herself in me as if I were
a costume. We stay like this,
intimate and murderous and grieving
in her thick dark world
for months. We eat pomegranates
and drink cups of our own tears.
And when finally the earth cracks open
and I rise again into the outer
world it is with her eyes
that I see, she my blood sister,
horror, truth, the filled self.

The Infected Hand

—for Gia

It was where she had
shot up so much there
was a hole partly
scabbed over,
which she picked at
when she wanted
a direct line to the blood
stream, blood-flowers opening
all the way to the heart,
a wound to make the heart
warm, it was an early
announcement of her death,
which would take the year
to perform, a new opening
she had cratered into
the body, and I wanted
to bring her hand to my mouth
and kiss the new cankered mouth there,
speak to it, I wanted my words
to be blood-food
for the knotted infected heart,
the lungs thick with infection,
the staring eyes infected,
my voice entering
her body like a clean needle,
I understand.

Pain Killers

I love those drugs they give
to relax you, the kind gas
of the dentist, the mysterious
pills and shots before and after
surgery, you lie there
on the chair or the bed
like Christ, all your wounds
illuminated, vibrating
with existence:

               for this is what
those drugs do, they do not
kill pain, they illuminate it,
fertilize it, until you are
so aware that you are almost
numb, it is pain made so much
itself it doesn't seem like itself.

So there you are in the chair
thinking *I must cut the grass*
I must clean the house I
must read important books
and underline the important
parts, and then the drug
kicks in its sweetness

and your wrists that had been
tight with trouble, your wrists
that had shouted and shook
at your child, begin to warm and blush,

and your body relaxes. You lie there
like nothing, the pathways
to memory opening, you can feel
the doors opening in all the veins
of your body, the first touch,
the first disappointment,
now you can stand to think
about it, now you can remember it,
despair, bitterness fully clothed,
sweet grace, you hold it in your body,
try to make it last,
close your eyes

and remember

how your brother would take
this sweetness, how he took it
and took it until his eyes closed.

Our eyes do not close like his. We
are lying down in an office, we
are waiting for a dentist, a surgeon
to cut us open, deliver us.

Keeping the Roses Alive

—in memory, N. Sabin

1

The rose bushes were not mine,
never would I have planted such clichés
of daintiness and fragility, cultivated
so long for beauty that they had
lost all hope of strength.
But I decided to try to keep them alive.

I am a twenty-four hour nurse,
and they are my patients
sick and yellowed, but still living.

No other plant has so many enemies:
rose aphids, rose gall, rose chafers,
rose midges, rose scales, rose slugs,
rose stem borers, rose weevils;
Japanese beetles, red spider
mites, bronzing, brown canker, stem
canker, leaf rust, powdery mildew,
crown cell, innumerable nasty viruses,
and finally, black spot,
which can't be cured, although the books
say prevention with fungicide is possible:
cut off all the infected leaves, spray
on a weekly basis every bit of the rest
of the bush, don't forget under the leaves.

2

It must have been one mad cell
we didn't get, the doctor tells me.
Pruning the breasts is not always
100 percent effective. The two lumps,
black as black spot, in the lymph
glands, inoperable.

Later, I call myself up on the phone
to say how sorry I am to hear.
Doctors say six, maybe eight months
I tell me. My voice is slurred,
but numbly happy. I have
started drinking again, I say.
I will not undergo the fungicide,
I say. *I understand*, I say,
I would do the same.

This morning the rose bushes
pushed me too far. I drank
a coffee cup of bourbon,
pulled the fuckers up
by the roots.

How to Write a Poem

Write down four nouns. Then four verbs.
Make sure they are not related.
Then use them to write something you've
never written before, a secret, a terrible
secret. Make it up if you don't have one.
Make sure there is an even deeper secret
within the secret.

Rock. Pen. Hand. Earth.
Sing. Breathe. Bleed. Wrap.

What could I have done,
the passionate cancer already singing
in her lymph glands, the scooped out
tissue pulsing its truths.
The rock in my hand like a telephone
to anywhere but logic, the earth

breathing in my ear, what more would
my voice or pen bleeding regrets
and how sorrys. A year to watch
her die in, a year to wrap it up.

Ode to Caffeine

I have known the sadness of decaffeinated coffee,
thin, flat and tasteless as boiled tap water,
safe, bitter and boring as a marriage gone fat,
righteous and logical as a Republican,
and so I have done it, I have drunk
the coffee I stayed away from so long,
the thick dark coffee teeming with lovely
molecules of caffeine that rush up the blood,
heat up the heart beat, the molecules of caffeine
that fist womb and breasts with polyps and cysts,
and I'm happy as a train, I've got caffeine in my fingers,
in my brain, who cares if it lingers,
I'm saying no to life
without the warm electric feel of it on mornings
like this when life looks like a set of rules
made up by long-living fools, I'm saying I need it
to tickle me along to that good lack of stress,
that good young death.

Hacking Away the Wisteria

The wisteria had become wanton, exuberant,
triumphant, almost hysterical, breathing its way across
my mother's lawn, working its way underneath the shed through
the floor, willing itself through the ceiling and out
the window to the holly tree on the other side of the yard,
wrapping itself around everything in its way, the azaleas,
hibiscus, camellias, all caught in its stranglehold,
insidious, another summer neglected and it would
enter the house, sneak its green fingers into my
mother's bedroom, surround her body while she
slept, enter her like some ancient god,

or my father—
We planted it together long ago, she says.
See how it poisons the ground, she says.

She had tried to kill it several times,
claiming it had responded too well
to the climate, that it frightened her—
it's like a thing
from outer space, she tells me,
and I see she is frightened,
she is thinking about her death;
every time I visit she gives me
some thing from my childhood,
tells me something I need
to know for when she dies.

So I become the kind of son
she never had, a noble prince, the hacksaw
my sword. I set to, hacking away at
the wisteria. I make a big deal of it, the way
we always make much of something
easy enough to do, so that
it counts in our favor when the harder thing,
which we cannot do, comes up.

How much, how much
do you have to cut off to begin again,
would we ever do it
if we knew what we nurtured
would become weed—

Afterwards, I place a piece of it
with root in a pot. When I leave,
the wisteria hacked down,
I take it home with me,
plant it in my yard.

I plant it
as if it were a piece of my mother,
as if it were a piece of my father,
as if it were my mother's slow death,
my father's gangrenous leg, his shriveled liver,
and I watch daily to see
if it's taken root,
I imagine it in my dreams,
the first push of new root into
soft fresh soil, moist with waiting, *wildness,*

wisdom, weeping, wickedness,
word, woman, wish, welt, wailing,
wanting, withdrawing, wet, within,
whip, willful, willing, wind there is

no wisteria in me, no wisteria,
there is nothing
my son will have to hack out.

The Darkness of God: Leaving Louisiana

I carry His inner darkness around with me
on my face where everyone can see
the dark hair above my upper lip
and chin that gets darker and thicker
the older I get, as if I were becoming more
and more male as I approach death—
more and more my brother—*it's French,*
it's a sign of passion, my father would
say when I was younger, but I shaved it,
bleached it, plucked it
until my face was clean and smooth
like what I was: a young girl, innocent
but darkly passionate, with
sexed heart, inherited lusty bones
and eyes, even my eyebrows thick and lusty
with this black, bristly religion.

Mother says I'm not supportive
when all the deaths of brothers,
nephews and fathers occur, I bail out,
I desert, she cannot see how
I am becoming a swamp, she doesn't see
that a swamp supports nothing
but its own passion, and so I am leaving
the cypress trees, though I know well
their beauty, I am leaving the warm winters,
the hot food, I am leaving
the religion that announces
itself on my face each morning.

I have seen aunts and grand-
mothers, old and forgetful
of their faces, let the dark
hair on lips and chin grow
until they look like men,
the hair thick and black
as God. They walk around oblivious
of their mustaches and scraggly
chin-beards, because no one loves
them enough to tell them. This
is death, the tragic male of the family
coming through, God as family,
and I wonder if away from here
there will be One who will love me
enough to keep this dark grace
from my face, or will I die
old and marked like this,
only this hair to bless me,
to remind me of the darkness
of God, to remind me, at the moment
of death, who I am, from whence I came.

Thinking About Being a Woman As I Drive from Louisiana to New Mexico

I am driving through the night,
dusk settling on the road ahead
like a tired woman,
I am driving,
a woman possessed,

and as I drive I think of how
when you have driven many hours
and are slightly deprived of sleep,
thoughts bloom
madly in you, uncontrollable,
like azaleas in spring—

I think of the bougainvillea
I left on a pot on my porch,
how the man at the nursery
had told me to keep it
rootbound, that it wouldn't bloom
unless it was stressed out, those
were his words, *stress it out*,

as if cruelty were a necessary
condition for beauty.

Blossoms
of lotus feet, hips hysteric
from cinched in waists,

plucked eyebrows, shaved legs,
curlers in the hair at night, headaches,
pin scabs from the plucking, rashes
from the shaving, the mothers
in China breaking the feet of their daughters,
wrapping the bones of the feet
in perfumed bloodied bandages
night after night, the men smelling the feet,
the blood in the East from the clitorectomies,
the women made more desirable,
the mothers do it, the blood
is on the mothers' hands, the cutting,
the girdles, the bras, the tight stockings,
the highheels, the corsets, the women
who starve themselves, the women
throwing up, the women being tucked
and stitched and sucked
and reshaped—

Rootbound. I say it
over and over again
to the darkening road,
as if some clue to my life
were there. What would it
be like, one's roots twirling
round and round in a clay
pot, dark and moist, nowhere
else to go but round, now
touching now winding
and twisting, but always
in the same direction,
around and in around

and in until the root
itself becomes soil.

My mother who refuses to travel,
to be a woman like her,
always waiting
for something to arrive.

You've got to suffer if you want to be beautiful,
she would say, though she hardly needed to tell me,
I could feel it everywhere around me as I was growing up
like the way you can sometimes feel the darkness
gets a texture, takes shape, touches you all
over your naked body at night.
The girdles and longline bras
she spooned herself into, the first bra
she strapped me into—that
was the first time she said it to me,
reminded me of the little mermaid
who had to attach clams
to her tail when she turned fifteen.
It was in all the stories though, the sisters
who cut off their toes and heels to make
them small enough to fit the glass
slipper, the blood
filling the shoe like gold,
mirror mirror on the wall
who is most beautiful of all—

The night lies on the road
ahead, a rich carpet
or a tablecloth, or a sheet

I have to change,
and sometimes I wish
I could shake off my mother's sex
like a bad dream. As the hours
stretch and the dark becomes
darker and the fellow travelers
become fewer and fewer
and almost hallucinating
with lack of sleep and
pumped to exhaustion with
caffeine and sugar, I think
of how, like this, one can sense
the desperateness of night,
how a certain kind of music
could drive one
to almost anything at night.
I understand how murders
could be committed at night
by those perfectly sane in the day.
The way night enters you like a god,
Zeus and Leda, Europa, Danae,
Yahweh and Mary, like that—

My sister's friend,
raped last week in her car
by a man posing as a policeman
who pulled her over for weaving on the road.
I try to drive straight, watch
where I'm going, not break
any laws.

The time in Costa Rica
alone in the tent by the volcano,
the five men drunk
coming to swim at midnight,
stripping naked
in the moonlight,
the way I
clutched my knife
and didn't
sleep that night.

The time in New Orleans
the man who turned my
electricity off, waited behind the bush,
pulled the belt over my throat,
my voice, my scream all that saved me,
the gun I finally bought in Texas.

Maybe it is now that the animal,
armadillo, possum, something
large and slinky, appears
in my headlights like a messenger
from the night, already under
my tires, no time for swerving or stopping
or thinking. I hit it straight on,
sixty miles an hour,
feel the thud of tire against body,
feel the car lift a little like hope
then fall, then the back tire hit
and it's over. I'm gone.

Two cars behind me. Was it
hit again, and again? Was it
knocked over, back broken?
I don't stop, I don't go
back, what if I had a gun now,
would I be like a man,
would I go back
and see what I killed? Would
a man go back? I keep driving,
gripping the steering wheel, now ready
for any kind of light,
almost not breathing,

I have killed something,
but I keep driving, that is all
I know to do, keep driving,
roots ripped out and flying
back like streamers or bloomers
or bras, I am driving
away from and into my sex,
my light.

Autumn

What is left of the leaves on the trees
is a soup of light, a *frisson* of color.
It is their damage that is beautiful.

I look at myself in the mirror,
time's damage present in all seasons,
and wonder when I will see it as beauty.

And Scheherazade noticed that dawn was approaching and stopped telling her tale. Thereupon Dunazade said, "Oh sister, your tale was most wonderful, pleasant, and delightful!"

"It is nothing compared to what I could tell you tomorrow night if the king would spare my life and let me live."

"By Allah," the king thought to himself, "I won't slay her until I hear some more of her wondrous tales."

So they continued to rest in mutual embrace until daylight finally arrived. After this the king got up to perform his official duties, but he did not call upon the vizier to perform the execution. . . . That night he had his will of Scheherazade, as was his wont, and afterward, as they were relaxing, Dunazade came to her sister and asked her to tell another tale.

"With the king's permission," she said.

And Shahryar replied, "You have my permission."

So Scheherazade resumed her storytelling.

—*from* Arabian Nights, *tr. Jack Zipes*

2. Notes for the Beloved

I am walking into you
as if you were death,
a lake foreign and deep.
I have written out my will
given away my possessions
and I am not coming back
until I am changed.

I have never wanted to give anyone all
my strangenesses, my wild desires,
my holy and boring darkness.

But you have cut into me like a new river
and I am flowing away from myself and
into you, all joy all imperfection, I move
now more in your veins than in mine.

That your words take flight in the soil of my body,
enter me as one unknown, something
utterly other, devour, love me in that language,
it is prayer and ravishing at once,
the sounds call out alone,
unattached to meaning,
they call out their loneliness
speaking to guts and veins and heart,
the voice as beloved,
a spirit
that comes out of your mouth,
surrounds me, fills the room
with song, I am entering
the jungle again, I am only
body, only listening, only
vibration, only breath
opening to receive your lips,
your voice singing
its sweet, sweet
violences.

Listening to songs
of love, as if I were in love, or wanted
to be. The greatest disappointment:
that love does not last,
that we are not satisfied with this,
but keep on desiring it even though
we do not desire it. Love. Drugs.
Don't trust metaphor. Don't say it,
love is a drug, don't trust *is*,
look what a whore *is* is:
love is a cancer, love is a rock,
love is desperation, love is
fracture, love is failure,
a sentence fragment,
a comma splice, a dangling
modifier, a title
without a text, a deep error,
the unspoken last line
in a poem written by death.

Thinking About Herbs

This is how I rise in you,
a green breath of words,
a pungent aroma that
cries out until you bring the crushed
things to your face, inhale deeply.

That Death Come as the Beloved

All winter I thought about you
and *you*, all winter I thought
about death rhyming with
desire, and all winter
the safe sex reports on the public
radio station rang in my ears
like school bells calling me
to wake and study and weep,
calling me out of the body
and into a world without song—

My love, to choose
to touch you, to choose to
walk into you open-mouthed,
to touch tongues like angels
or children, to be wounded
by your seraphim lips,
to want to take your weeping
into me and make it joy,
to want you to slip out,
weeping with that joy,
spilling it back into me,
to be in the beloved
as in a foreign country,
the tongue elated at speaking
a new language,
the new sun's blood burning
in you like a hot hot pepper,

lungs screaming for air
like a child's first breath
as it becomes irrevocably
other, a rarefied, rich air
that smells like Europe,
wine, a spiced white
grape air, like nothing
you have ever ever smelled
or tasted before—

To trust you
is to trust a swamp
of faces, bodies,
darknesses terrifying
and wondrous, black
and luminous as the Past—

I would wade into that love
gladly, thick, viscous as first day's
blood, heavy with knowing,
I would become that blood,
liquid matter, as in the womb,
I would lie down in it,

I would die
even the most horrible
of deaths,
let the throat go black
and the skin, the eyes
shrivel and peel like
things struck by lightening,

but I would have the gift
of your body, the fruit
of it fully in my mouth
and my emptied hands.

I would choose
death as I chose
you, I would walk,
open-eyed and bare-
chested, into winter,
I would reach inside
to grip the marrow of you,
I would take your death
into me like a holy disease
that drinks in my body
until it is drunk
and I rise from your side
and into another life.

October

For beauty is nothing
but the beginning of terror. . . .
                    Rainer Maria Rilke

The leaves of the sugar maple blanket
the dry creek, reds bleeding into oranges
and yellows, a mess of melodrama.
There is such beauty in dying,
I want October to go on doing it.

Because of October light
shadows grow longer, darker—
you cannot shake your own,
whose sharpness startles you.

Like the flowers who linger through this month,
you can't believe in the possibility of winter.

❖ ❖ ❖

The flowers are brave, to bloom now.
They are various and plentiful:
sturdy goldenrod lights the creek bed,
illuminating its emptiness. Curry-
colored Maximilian sunflowers
grow each flower on top of the last,

49

a totem pole of flower faces.
You have to cut up the stems
to separate the flowers.

The leaves on the trees,
the great clichés of autumn,
are like us, brittle, ready
to fall off. They brush against each other
in the wind, still making a whispery music,
colored for escape.

When I found the pile of bodiless
butterfly wings, mostly Monarchs,
at the place where the creek splits
and there is a show of milkweed,
I wanted to scream.

There was something horrible about the way
the wings were untouched, perfectly intact,
laid out as if accidentally dropped
from some collector's case.

I wanted there to be more evidence
of destruction.

Autumn lies over the land
like your body over mine.
Its colors and shadows twist
like roots into all that is tender.

January

A train lets people out,
then goes off, it does not
care about anything.

We run into a phone booth
with our familiar lips.

I do not know how it happens that I grow in you again.

What are my lips?
Harmonica I want you
to play until breath
is gone to song

To see, finally, where you had lived, were born: these Yorkshire
moors in winter—startlingly
cold, wind like death, bleak and fertile wasteland:

                    Homeless:

Night fills you
like winter
a banquet

your lips

cool and full
as the darkness
I taste in my mouth
when we kiss.

No Tomatoes

The tomato plants won't have sex;
though they are healthy and green,
large and thickly vined,
yellow-flowered and ready
for it, they do not grow fruit;
the flowers shrivel after a while
and fall off. And I don't understand;
the sun is full and gentle, the soil
well-prepared. I have watered and withheld
water; I have pruned and stalked,
hand-picked bugs and fought off slugs,
walking around at night like a thief
with a flashlight. I have even tried
hand fertilization, masturbating
each flower with a Q-tip
but to no avail. They remain uninterested.

And I can't help but think of us
in this greenhouse of a house,
love and clean sheets,
privacy and diaphragms,
health and black lingerie,
but we lie separate and disinterested
under the warm prodding of a sweet June night.
Our bodies are green and leafy, we smell
of growth, our hands are ripe
with the viney smell of tomato
plant, but there is nothing

like desire here, nothing
like a warm tomato picked almost
overripe off the vine, so red
you could cry, so full of juice
and flavor that salt and pepper
seem heresy.

No, there are no tomatoes here, no one to tell
me why, and I do not know

what kind of interference
it will take
to want each other again.

Sestina for the Beloved

I would wake at night to their breath, the sound of them together,
their want,
the smell of their thighs and bones,
even thousands of miles away I could feel him undress
her, could hear his voice speaking
her name. It is not my name, which is difficult.

What he had with the two of us was not difficult,
it was as easy as night's breath,
as easy as me not speaking,
not saying what it was I wanted
most, not saying I wanted to undress
only for one man, only for one to know the bones

of me, the bones of my mouth, the bones
of my feet, of my heart, even the difficult
bones of my eyes and sex, only one to undress
my voice, only one to sing my breath,
only one to know the forest of my want,
to know there is only one who is speaking

my name in dreams, speaking
my body as if even voice had bones.
What I want is uncompromising, what I want
is difficult,
is like wanting water to offer breath,
is like wanting fire to undress

itself, is about possession undressing
itself, is about what it means to be speaking
at all, is about belonging like breath
to the beloved, the one whose bones
are inside you like so many difficult
hearts, the only one you want to want

so much that all there is of living is that want.
I cannot tell you it will be easy to undress
your heart only for me, that I will not be difficult,
that some days and nights you may feel as if you are speaking
to no one, that some nights your bones
won't ache for the touch of another, the sweet breath

of the unknown, the undressed breath
of one less difficult, a bone-
want that I will recognize, whose ache I will honor and sweeten
     with my love, my many, many breaths.

. . . *the* Nights *are nothing without the nights.*

—*Sir Richard Francis Burton, notorious translator of the unexpurgated* *version of* **Arabian Nights.**

3. Eight Nights of Fantasies

The First Night

THE INVITATION

It is August and even the moon
is hot, a white cake
baking in the night.

Two thousand miles gone,
how to bind him, how make
him taste this cake.

This is my canoe, we
are paddling into the moon
slipping over warm-worded
water like black glass, under
sentences of cypress trees hung
with gray moss lungs
of stories never told.

The night is sex, a woman
with full thighs, a woman
who smells of apples, a woman
lying on her back, carnal
mushroom, the air
is heavy, the hot weight of a man
you can taste,
his hands that smell of garlic and wine,
his breath is food, I want
to devour him, I am paddling,
I am undressing into moon,

this is an office, this is a bedroom,
this is a boat, this is a baseball field,
this is a church, a card game,
I can take or be taken, I can
punish or be punished, I am she
who tells stories to stay alive,
come to me and I will let you wrap
a rope around my wrists and I will tell
what I dream, what I breathe,
what I think when I bleed, when I come
in the mouth of the moon.
Roped to night, I will make
this the rope that binds you to me.

Hot and glowing like trust
moon's blood-light will cover us.
We will paddle into it,
and we will breathe.

The Second Night

PUTANA

*The name of wife may seem more sacred or more binding, but sweeter for me
will always be the word mistress, or, if you will permit me, that of concubine or
whore. God is my witness that if Augustus, Emperor of the whole world,
thought fit to honor me with marriage and conferred all the earth on me to
possess for ever, it would be dearer and more honorable to me to be called not
his Empress but your whore.*

Heloise to Abelard

That your words
could transform me,
could speak in my bones
could run in my veins
from head to breath
that I could love from your lips
even a name like *putana*—

whore, woman
wholly sexed

die, you tell me, over and over,
dai, dai, dai, and I try, as if
your words were fingers
and tongue.

That I could want these words
that call me so fully and seductively
to whoredom, disaster,
heaven.

The Third Night

THE DIFFERENCE BETWEEN LUST AND DESIRE

The woman is tired of her husband
but she is bound to him with children.
They mate quickly in the dark
like miserable animals, she
hears his breathing afterwards
it sounds like a stone, a mountain,
a faithful dog.
                        You see,
the clitoris is not unlike the cock:
it raises itself unbidden with sorrow,
moves one to couple with whatever
is there.

The one she desires has a name
she whispers over and over
at night as if he were plural as if
he were with her, she would drink
his breath she moves
toward his lips
like we paddle into
the moon his absence
that makes her
words her swamp.

The Fourth Night

WHILE BEING FED

It is not enough to say
the moon is a cake.
She demands food,
real food. It is morning, spring,
green with birds and new leaves.
He brings her cereal and milk.
She demands to be eaten
as well as fed, so his mouth
and tongue sip at her
between spoonfuls of cereal.
Later he gives her a bowl of black-
berries he has picked
and fresh cream he has whipped.
His hands are large as her hunger
and scratched from the brambles as
if something were written there
and she brings one of them to her mouth
like something holy
she touches her lips
to his palm.

The Fifth Night

WHEN SHE MASTURBATES

First of all she eats jellybeans,
a pile of about seven
different colors in her hand.
To get in the mood. *He will come
home soon, any day now.* She lies
down, no music, the sweetness
of jelly beans in her teeth
like rubber sugar, she licks her fingers—
I touch myself to find him she
thinks of faceless men who have his face
te quiero, one of them says. It is sweet
to come by imagining coming,
sweeter still to think of him
sucking the sweet swollen bean
between her legs
until it melts.

The Sixth Night

WHAT SHE DREAMED OF EASTER NIGHT

It wasn't a dream. He came to me,
wet from the river, his clothes
torn and smelling like smoke,
Mexico, mesquite, his breath
chile, he walked into my
bedroom in boots full of mountain
and desert, he was wet earth
and he bent over me, apologized
for taking so long, I heard him,
he had ridden three days and nights
his horse stamped and snorted
outside my window *¿me quieres?*
he asked, and I asked
myself if I were dreaming when he
threw his hat to the night, but
I could feel the shape of his head,
the muscles of his neck and back
as he kissed me, my lips weeping,
my lips being pressed against
my teeth, his tongue cool
and sweet as spring water in my
mouth I could feel him all meat
and desire and I smelled horse
when he entered me and I knew
what had been between
his legs three days as he

galloped into this same moon,
and then he rose and that is why
I am alone this morning, skin
smelling of smoke and horse,
lips stunned, body branded.

The Seventh Night

IN THE JUNGLE

Beyond his words I see
the jungle, and the red
oozing resin hardening
on the Bleeding Tree. I see
rain on leaves, a parrot snake,
but none of this changes
anything: the wiseman has proclaimed
to all of the tribe that I will
never have children

and my beloved will not be allowed
to marry me, and I cannot bear the stares
of others so I run into the deepest
green of the jungle, into and over
giant tree ferns thorns leaves and beetles
crackling like the bones of my heart
underneath my feet I am shedding
myself as I run the better to become
forest, honey, breadfruit, weevil
golden beetle flag
bug monkey howling anything
other than human other than
woman whose breasts ache and swing
who wants to tear her heart out
hold it triumphant above her

head *I will become fungus star*
fish fungus birds nest fungus
cup fungus I throw myself
down to the floor of the jungle
my heart beating the smell
of leaves of dark rotted forest
bottom in my nose and mouth and he
catches me up, he turns me around
and I open, I let him cut me take out
my heart and eat it as I have
eaten his, he is I am everything
I see, wild ginger bird of paradise
climbing pepper vine pitcher plant
thornbug liana rafflesia
all plants that hang and twist
and creep and climb
their way to make this jungle,
our kisses and sighs and dampness
and breath and wanting all part of
it all things that must die like
this place for no good reason
but the world's will.

The Eighth Night

IN THE GALAPAGOS ISLANDS

I am brown wheat
the sun hot in my body,
I am lying on top
of a small fishing boat,
I am wanting to be fucked
by the sky, as if it could gather
itself into a shape,
I am thinking of the quickness
of the birds' mating on the islands
how I don't want that,
I am thinking of the long scar
on the leg of my guide from the *macho*
sea lion, sinking its mouth into
her flesh, to be bitten like that,
is that what I want,

and could sex evolve into something
wholly other here, could he come
to me as sky or ocean, as emptiness,
as thought, as animal, could I
embrace him in this sun that
made me brown, could our mating
become these islands,
volcanic isolate teeming
with beauty, strangeness.

4. And a Song from Death

Death, on Vacation, Tends Her Garden

I love that greening in spring in the mouth of the sun,
the way the earth sings here, not dark but green
with me. And the bees, the way they separate
the petals of flowers
with such gentleness and sureness,
what I would give
to have a beloved like a bee!
To love like that
I would die myself.

And I love the way seeds
break open in the earth unseen
and breathe themselves
into air, the way leaves unfurl
like flags from young stems weak
as mortal lives, I could break them
with a hard rain,

the way they are like human lips,
those first leaves opening,
and I love the way the weeds cry tragically
to get in, as relations at funerals,

the stout herbs with their fragrances
that come from being bruised,
I love them too,
the way grief turns to scent,
the way regret becomes soil,
black loam—

here am I loved, here am I love,
here, my voices, eyes, mouths, skins,

here, the place I betray
what I am.